THE SOUND OF A CREATURE'S WINGS SPREADING

an anthology of writing created during the Summer Writing Challenge 2021

compiled by Kibriya Mehrban

The following pieces were written in response to prompts given by Liz Berry and Fiona Joseph during the Spark Summer Writing Challenge 2021 which took place online from Monday 26th July – Friday 30th July 2021.

About Writing West Midlands

Writing West Midlands evolved from the work of the Birmingham Book Festival, established in 1999.

The organisation is now the literature development agency for the region. We achieved National Portfolio Organisation status from Arts Council England in 2012; an important step which confirmed our strategic role in building the sector's diversity and resilience.

Writing West Midlands now provides a wide range of services for writers and readers, including our Spark Young Writers programme, our Room 204 Writer Development scheme, the Birmingham Literature Festival and the West Midlands Readers' Network.

COPYRIGHT

ISBN 979878178-596-4

Spark Young Writers is a Project of
Writing West Midlands

Edited by Liza Riemann &
Kibriya Mehrban

With thanks to:
Liz Berry
Fiona Joseph
Will Smith
George Bastow
&
Heddwen Creaney

Contents

Day One: KEYS

We asked our young writers to create a story, poem or piece of descriptive writing involving an imagined key.

An Unwanted Inheritance
Erin Oakley

Through the net curtains, the morning sunrise looked much the same as the glow from the gas streetlamps. This made it very difficult for me — even though several months had elapsed since the death of my father — to tell whether it was morning when I awoke. As an occasional insomniac and all-round poor sleeper, there had been more than one instance when I had woken up and got completely dressed without realising that it was still the middle of the night.

It was because of this that I had developed the habit of opening the curtains as soon as I awoke, just to make sure I didn't have to go back to bed.

So, still bleary eyed, this morning as on any other, I climbed out of bed and threw back the curtains. I ended up blinking against the morning light that assaulted my retinas. They had been hoping for an excuse to go back to sleep.

Having established that I wasn't wasting my time, I closed the curtains, lit a candle, and began to get dressed. All of my clothes were too big; my father had been a full two feet taller than me before old age weighed him down. Every item of clothing had ten years' worth of holes in them, patched with varying levels of efficacy and in a multitude of colours. It was the only part of the inheritance I had really needed, yet the least impressive. In the half-light, I managed to find a shirt — sickly yellow in colour, with patches in varying shades of grey and white — and pulled it on, before scrambling for some trousers. When I finally found some, I thanked the relevant powers that they were a dark enough shade that you couldn't see the stains.

Even when dressed in the least shabby sets of clothes, I looked less like the heir to a manufacturing fortune than the man who carried his bags.

That suited me just fine. While my father had loved money so much that at times he had seemed like a particularly tight-fisted magpie, I had lost my taste for it after I realised I could have all the fun I wanted on a low-ranking civil servant's salary. I ought not to have had to get a job, but since my father's love for money outweighed his love for his son, I was refused an allowance.

I groped in the shadows for the door key I had deposited safely on my dresser the previous evening. Although there was no longer any reason for me to do it, I hadn't quite been able to shake the habit of locking my door before I went to sleep: it had been a matter of life and death in my previous lodgings. Not so much now, but I couldn't get to sleep otherwise.

It was too dark for me to find the key, no matter how hard I tried, so I opened the curtains again. The key was nowhere to be seen.

It must have fallen down the back of the dresser.

I crouched down to look beneath the dresser and my eyes caught the glint of metal. Except, when I stuck my hand out to grab the key, I touched instead the iron grid of the air vent.

"I can't believe this," I muttered under my breath. "I need that key. I can't be stuck in this room. I can't."

A soft, tinkling noise came out of the vent and slowly resolved itself into a voice. "And why should I give it to you, live one?"

I sighed. No matter how hard I tried, I really couldn't get my head round the fact that the only functional bedroom in this entire damned mansion was haunted.

I hadn't believed it at first. When the servants had refused to enter, I had been certain that it was a subtler kind of strike, on account of the fact my father had barely paid them enough to live off. However, even after I had increased their wages — so that they were the best paid servants in the entire city — they would still clutch their crosses as they walked past the doorway. They wouldn't touch anything that had been in the room, unless it had been cleaned thoroughly beforehand. And they certainly wouldn't carry a key for the door.

Eventually, I had begun to notice odd things that I couldn't really explain. The curtains would move in a non-existent breeze. Books I hadn't touched in months would lie open on the floor, removed carefully from their piles. My clothes would move into different drawers. The floorboards would creak as though someone was walking over them, even though I was the only person to come into the room.

After that, I had stopped trying to convince them that they were wrong. But I had refused to cave to their insistence that I refurbish one of the other rooms so I could move. I did my own cleaning and washed all of my teacups thoroughly before handing them back to the cook. When I replaced the lock on the door, I didn't bother to get the key copied.

So, I had two options: I could shout out of the window and hope that someone was kind enough to send someone burly enough to break the door down, or I could try and bargain with the ghost that seemed to have taken possession of the key.

Safe to say, I tried the shouting first.

Almost everyone ignored me. Those who didn't shouted obscenities or threw stones. My father had not been a popular man, and no matter how hard I tried, I was not going to be able to reverse fifty years of resentment in a couple of months.

Swearing under my breath, I sat down next to the dresser.

"What do you want for the key?" I said, in a voice that I hoped didn't sound condescending.

The vent made a noise as though it was considering. "I want you to talk to me. Tell me about your life. Tell me about other people's lives. Tell me about the new animals they have at the zoo. Read me books. Read me newspapers. I really don't care what it is you tell me about. You cannot imagine how dull it is to be a ghost. It takes all my energy just to ruffle the curtains. You don't know how lucky you are."

"That's all?" I immediately regretted saying it, worried that it might provoke a request for human sacrifices. I had read my fair share of *Penny Dreadful*s, but ghosts were not my area of expertise. I wasn't entirely sure that I had an area of expertise, but if I did, I was certain it wouldn't be ghosts. Perhaps that was about to change.

"Well, I'd prefer not to have to share my room with you: you keep putting things down on top of me. But I've seen the state of the other rooms in this monstrosity, and there's enough black mould to turn you into a ghost."

"Right. I suppose I can start fixing up the house, god knows there's enough money. It might be a while until I'm out of your hair though." It felt rather like I was talking to an aunt I didn't know very well. "If you don't mind me asking, what did you do to make the servants so afraid?"

"Oh, that… I got fed up with your father being such a misery guts and knocked his chamber pot onto his bed just as the maid was removing it to clean it."

I couldn't quite stifle my laugh. "Was he very angry?"

"Deathly."

"So, I agree to your terms. Could I possibly have that key back now?"

There was a clunking sound, like the noise a train makes as it pulls into a station, and then the key flew out of the vent and into my waiting hand. I had never been so pleased to feel the cool, unremarkable brass against the skin of my hand.

As I unlocked the door and walked out into the hallway in search of food, I could picture a sign in my head:

Joseph Baker
Ghost Negotiator
No ghost too belligerent.

The Key
Fanni Doroti Polgar

Have you ever wondered what it would feel like to possess the key to the most incomprehensible, momentous and cathartic place?

A key, small in size and a threadbare chestnut in colour, with a pair of silver wings sleeping on either side of its centre patiently sits an arm's length from your reach. Yet, with every move, moment and memory, it goes unseen and untouched. Neglected. Unacknowledged to the extent that it might as well not exist at all.

There is, however, something distinctive and fundamental about the key's existence: You are the only person who it unveils itself to. You and you only can see it, hold it, and open the door to which it does belong…

The door, standing as tall as you in height, and ligneous in appearance, resembles the features of its interior, a relief from the initial enigma… A recklessly carved heart stabbed into the centre jumps out at a primary glimpse, followed by an unkempt yet unmissably light-emitting piece of paper, visibly torn from an old notebook. The note is tattooed with the word 'dreams' and stems from a family portrait which lies plastered across the bottom of the door; a band aid preventing two of the four corners of the frame from partitioning. Finally, some subtle and some heavy footprint-like marks decorate the remaining areas and lead to the keyhole, which whispers "welcome" in the most elegant, captivating, yet humble tone.

Can you see the key?

Can you hear the welcome?

If not, be patient…

Nobody can open this door for you, nobody can hand you the key. Nobody can walk into this room for you because this room is *you*. Your truth, your love, your loss, your light, your regrets, the masked emotion, the secret devotion: your entire life.

If we all opened our doors, held our keys, understood ourselves and became open to opening every door we've worked a lifetime to close, then who is to say there wouldn't be more peace and liberty?

The key is yours to hold, and the door is

yours to open.

So, see it, hear it, grasp it, and take hold of it as though the rest of your life depends on it. Because it does...

Ouroboros
Luca Rezzano

This piece of writing was inspired by the prompt 'Keys'. I initially considered how the shape or design of a key could be used within the story to create a dangerous atmosphere which is largely overlooked by the protagonist as a result of their own desire for change.

What it meant for me to be in possession of the key, I did not yet know. What I knew for certain was that uncovering this convoluted passport had rescued me from another afternoon of traipsing through the tawny halls of the bygone library where I so frequently found myself. Abandoning momentarily the opportunity to consider the origin of such a peculiar object or why, of all people, it had found its way to me, sun-deprived fingers began to wrap tightly around the handle. The single gemstone eye on the twisted snake's face stared up at me and I was overcome with wonder and rendered without sense.

       "James?" an echoing voice ricocheted on

the oak panels to my unwary ears, causing me to jump slightly, grasping the key with a new possessiveness, "Did you find that book you were asking about?"

I was attacked by the overwhelming fear that if I were to not move rapidly to discover the door, likely equal in grandeur, I might never escape the boundless monotony of my life.

"James?"

She was closer now.

With nowhere else to turn, I darted behind a velvet curtain, which had always appeared out of place in the deadened room. I tried my best to not shake with the fear of being discovered while the librarian marched inches from me. The sound of my own breath boomed around me, until another sense blighted my confined surroundings: the spinel gem in the eye of the key I still held burned as ferociously as a bonfire in my left hand, lighting up an engraved handle beside me.

Disguised by the scarlet curtain stood a door twice the size of any other in the library. The furious glow revealed complex engravings I did not at first understand: scenes of twisted beasts and humans. All were guarded by the bodies of two snakes, creating handles on both doors. I recoiled as much as the curtain allowed me to at the realism of the sculptures. For as long as I could remember, snakes had been my greatest fear, their ability to move so swiftly, to wrap themselves around their prey with such strength, to bite into the flesh and to suffocate. Holding up the key to the beady eyes of one, I was hit with the overwhelming realisation that in these few minutes I had uncovered both the key and its door, a perfect pythonic pair.

The clatter of shoes became fainter, and I reluctantly dared to let the curious handles leave my sight as I peered around the side of the curtain. The room was empty; here was my chance.

Hastily, I felt around between the heavy coils for the guarded keyhole and after a few moments, my fingers paused over a cavity. I held up the key as if it were merely a torch in order to see clearly my means of passage. Without a second of thought, I pushed the key into the lock to discover the secrets which I had, for weeks, walked unknowingly past.

Finally, I felt, my summer had some purpose.

Counterfeit Knowledge
Sadeen Ahmad

coffee-coloured hairs with lemon, beady eyes
the dominant presence of an owl pulsating in a
        delicate key.
smirking thorns warping around, like a serpent.
the key to a book of knowledge.

with recognition of your notability,
hushed and discreet whispers will reverberate,
the nocturnal animal will repeat its clues,
murmuring, *take the path to the home range.*

treacherous escapades and vigorous running.
who said getting to your bearing would be
        painless?
the thorns now snagging you: snatching your
        endurance.
the owl still hissing *take the path to the home range.*

you lay, unstirring and breathless.
every aspiration of unearthing knowledge seeping
        out,
like filthy water from a saturated cloth.
yet the bird-of-night's lemon, beady eyes still glow
        in the darkest moments.

drained, yet with drops of rejuvenation you carry
        on.

here you are: in the home range.
fluttering feathers drop like rain: pearly or tawny.
your heart palpitating wildly,
internally screaming at how you ultimately
        succeeded.
the moment you blink, owls scramble and pelt.
unravelling in the shape of a gnarled but
        monumental tree.
as you step forward, your hand trembles, holding
        the key.
the key that took you to the path of the home
        range.

there lay a petite box: its keyhole almost drawing
        and sucking you in.
the delicate key clasped tightly in your sweaty
        hand, slips.

slips out your hand and perfectly into the keyhole,
        like its locksmith intended.
elegantly turning until the satisfactory click!

with a heave, you open it.
but it turns out empty and abandoned.
you realise this was all counterfeit.
but then, the owls shove you into the box.

you hear a click.
and then everything spirals into sheer black.

The Key
Petra Rihan

It was beginning to get dark out, which gave me all the more reason to try and go as fast as possible. My little Mini was not built for these thin, treacherous country roads, and I was getting fed up. Every bump made me want to turn around and go home.

But I had to do this.

My grandmother died a few weeks back and left me her home. One may find that a surprise but she never liked her kids. They were a nuisance to her. She didn't have any siblings and her children (other than my mother) never had any kids. But Gran always took an interest in me. When I was younger, and mum was still alive, Gran would come to our small townhouse for a few days every three years. She'd take me in, tell me about her family and tell me stories. But that was the past; now I'm driving to a house I know nothing about, and my future is unclear.

Thankfully, I see a sign I've been looking for ahead of me: 'Fairview Woods'.

I see a gate and my jaw drops. In the will, the house was described as a 'modest cottage with a fair bit of land' but this... Grand charcoal gates stand, overgrown, drowned in plants that run into every small nook and cranny. Fog lines the ground and the sun is setting. Not a soul is around for miles, surely. What lies behind is the gates is a driveway to a majestic, grand old manor.

Grounds surround the manor, and it all feels so.... regal. So old. I never knew grandma was so rich. I wish I could tell mum, but she passed away too, recently. I heard her voice in my head and I chuckled gently: She'd say, 'Who knew that old bag could keep a secret as big as this? She was always one to brag. Isn't that right, Lizzy?'

I step out of my car and fumble for the key. A big key, fragile and ugly. I turn it in the lock and push the gates. They creak noisily, amidst the loud silence. I quickly drive up the driveway, heart pounding. A million questions rush through my head. My hands shake.

'How will I keep this house intact?'
'Is there reception for my phone?'
And finally, the one I'm trying to push away:
'Why do I not feel... Alone?'

Getting out of my car once again, I walk up the steps to a magnificent, dark mahogany old wood door. The house scares me. It feels as if it is looking down on me, judging me. I turn the key once again and can't help but think this key, this door, is leading me to something eerie, something… unsafe.

The door slowly swings back, heavy in its frame. I place the key on a chest of drawers by the door and fight through cobwebs. The house is darkly lit; it feels strange. Pictures are on the drawers and paintings on the walls. This was someone's home once.

Glorious, large stairs lead up to more floors.

I slowly make my way through the rooms. A living room, dining room, kitchen and halls. The wind whistles through cracks in the walls and my heart continues to pound. I feel like I'm being watched…

Old walls creak with memories, and tapping sounds on the window make me jerk my head to look around the sitting room I'm in. Something is not right. I walk over to a photo of Grandma and pick it up carefully.

That's when I hear it.

Footsteps.

Whispering.

A breath on my neck.

The photo falls from my hands and shatters on the floor.

Cold fingers on my back…

Grandma died here.

And I don't think she ever left.

For that key has led me somewhere I should not be.

And I am not alone.

The Recovered Diary of Mr S.

Blake Scammell

June 19ᵗʰ 2015

June 19th 2015

It was when the key was pulled clear of the water that I knew something was going to happen.

I was strolling along the riverbank, minding my own business, when I heard the sound of engines. A large river trawler, the type that sifts through the mud lining the riverbed like a thick, disgusting blanket to see what fortunes they can unearth. Usually a thankless job, it was one I had not yet considered, despite drawing closer to the age where I would be expected to take a job. I was not yet *that* desperate.

The trawler was stationary, sifting through the muck onboard. I was passing by when I saw a heavy, barnacle-encrusted key pulled clear of the river's embrace. A few moments later, it was returned to its watery grave and thrown overboard, but I heard it coming and caught it on the way down.

The weight of it unbalanced me and nearly sent me into the river. Staggering under the weight, I peered through the encrusted armour, trying to make out the original colour. Through the encrusted surface, I could just about make out a rich, hearty, relatively unspoiled bronze hue. I have decided to take the key home and to try to remove the outer coating, so that the original key can be used again.

June 21st 2015

Today was quite a strange day. I think I'll start from the beginning.

I finally finished cleaning the key of barnacles in my attempt to see its true appearance. I was not disappointed.

The key is the size of a normal key but is about the weight of two dictionaries, and made completely out of bronze. It has weird swirling patterns going across its entire length, and the patterns look vaguely ancient Celtic. In fact, judging by the quantity of barnacles on it, I would guess that's the era it originated from. Upon closer inspection, it had a finely detailed and engraved seahorse head at one end, and a jagged key end at another. In the midsection of the key were an additional three keyholes, all of which were different shapes and sizes.

After inspecting the mysterious key, I put it away in my safe and logged onto my computer. I went about my usual business, checking emails, sending emails, and doing other things, when I heard a loud *crack*. I spun around to see the safe door swung open and the key gone. There were numerous scorch marks on the door of the safe, and it was hot when I touched it. I searched for the key, but to no avail.

I will have to come to terms with its loss. I was quite attached to that key.

June 22nd 2015

I woke up at three in the morning. I found the key lying at the foot of the bed, glowing faintly in the darkness. When I tried to pick it up, a voice with a metallic edge to it rang out, saying "*Leave me. I am not yours to take.*"

When I looked at the key it was glowing more intensely. I lay back down and the glow softened. I am beginning to wonder if I am overworking myself.

June 23rd 2015

I started today by picking up the key to assure my troubled mind that the key didn't have a mind of its own. However, as soon as I went near the key I heard the voice again. I was unable to make out what it said this time, because the key spoke in Celtic, or some ancient language that has long been forgotten. I suddenly felt lightheaded and went outside. Then I blacked out.

I woke up with the key around my neck, a bulletin about a hypnotized fool stealing three antique keys blaring on the television, and saw three keys sitting on the table next to me. I tried to get up, but the key laid heavily on my chest. I could not move anything but my arms.

"Unlock me and I'll set you free" growled the key.

I felt strangely compelled to do so. I inserted the three keys into the keyholes on the bronze key, and it began to glow once more. I am writing this entry as the glow envelopes the room. I am not sure what will happen next...

Day Two: EMOTIONS

We asked our young writers to write piece of fiction or non-fiction fuelled by emotion. They could write a piece about a character who was feeling something intensely or write on a subject they had strong feelings about.

Fear
Chloe Pick

Today was going to be amazing. I was going to Disneyland with all my friends. We queued up to get our tickets then walked through the gates. We all decided to go on Hyperspace Mountain first, just so the queues didn't get too long, like they usually did. Everyone was so excited to be going on the ride, especially when the queue was tiny. But I couldn't ignore the sick feeling in my stomach. As we got closer to our turn, my friends began to notice that I wasn't as sure about getting on this ride as they were.

'Ella, come on the ride, it'll be fun.'

'Yeah, Ella, come on!'

I couldn't hear anything; it was like I was in a bubble – like I was detached from the world as my friends tried to reassure me. But I couldn't focus on that. I couldn't go on that ride… it was too big… And tall… and there– there was a big drop. I couldn't. I just couldn't. I know that it's safe but there are other rides that I could go on.

Rides that weren't so tall… with big drops… and lots of loop-the-loops. I could hear all my friends laughing around me: they were all having lots of fun at Disneyland. I wasn't. But it wouldn't hurt just to try, would it?

'Ella, come on! It's our turn, come on!'

'Yeah, yeah, I'm coming, let's go.'

I don't know why I said that. Why did I say that? As we went up the ride tracks, I could only think of the sudden drop on the other side. My breathing became shallow. I couldn't do this… but it was too late to get off now… and we were at the top. There was a countdown. I could barely hear. I could only see the drop just seconds away. I was going to die. There was no doubt about that.

'Ella, are you ok?'

I couldn't even reply to my friends. This was horrible… I was going to be sick. I couldn't hear the intense music being pumped into the air. Then we dropped. I was going to die. I was going to die. I was going to die. Goodbye cruel world.

Somehow I survived… but the ride had only just begun. Three loop-the-loops loomed ahead of me. I closed my eyes but that didn't stop the sense of vertigo as we sped around the loops. Why did I come on this ride when I could've just waited at the gate? Why didn't I just do that? I screamed as we were stopped, hanging upside down. We had stopped. We were stuck. We were going to die.

And then all of a sudden we were racing back into where we started. I got off the ride, my legs shaking like jelly, fear etched into my eyes. That haunted look probably wouldn't leave me for a while. I threw up, covering the ride operator. Then we went to the park first aid centre. Going on that ride was just a huge mistake. So much for a great day out.

Web
Luca Rezzano

*This piece was inspired by the prompt 'Emotions'.
Although I chose to explore several feelings in my
writing as it developed, particularly shame, I had
begun by using the idea of loneliness and isolation.*

It was as though there was a hole in my chest, an unending emptiness which would follow me until the end of my life, an isolation which no amount of attention could shake. The four cold walls which confined me to my reality felt miles away; even they did not wish to be associated with me. I felt my eyes dart around looking for any source of comfort.

How had I been made to feel this way? Why of all people–

I became aware of a dull light, illuminating a small patch of beige carpet in the dismal room. I half expected it to be an empty social media notification, encouraging me to stay up to date with the perfect and exciting lives of people I scarcely knew. I hoped, however, for a reminder that somebody still knew that I existed. From where I lay on the floor, I extended my arm out to the rectangular distraction, praying without faith that somebody would break my isolation.

You ok?

I gazed down at the message blankly, my heart sinking. Knowing I was unable to reply genuinely to such a question only increased my pain. It was a question so complex and yet so barren, not the lifeline I was hoping for. Of course, I understood that I could not burden another person, a friend, with my current circumstance – 'a problem shared is a problem doubled' as my grandmother had so often reminded me.

As I prepared to type an acceptable response, I was weighed down by the understanding that my reluctance to share what had happened was not just to spare another person the mental anguish, but to spare myself the reliving of my shame.

Shame. What is shame? The feeling of suffocating humiliation at one's own actions, but then what had I done, truly? No, this feeling was not shame. Not anymore at least.

Again, my mind was washed blank by a fresh wave of desolation crashing against the shores of my soul, eroding my hope. There was no possibility of me escaping this room, this great palace of nothingness of which I was both king and slave. In any case, it had been the world outside of my fortress which had betrayed me, leaving me with only this prison-like sanctuary. It was out in the world that I was vulnerable which, to me, felt far harsher than the security of my unending despondency.

The light was brighter this time, just inches from my eyes.

I heard about what happened... Please talk to me.

If the walls surrounding me were in the habit of cracking, then surely the sender's earnestness would have shone through them, however they were not. What did seep in like black mould was the realisation that the events of my day and the days before were being unravelled without my permission. **I heard about what happened**. It caused me to wheeze, and I was no longer able to hide my dread. I was trapped like a spider beneath a glass, unable to escape the many sets of impatient eyes and their suffocating glare. These once-tough walls had become transparent.

It got harder to breathe, it was as though everyone was staring at me like a struggling specimen on a dish, but despite their watch, ultimately, I was alone. With anxious fingers I began to craft a response: **I don't think that I can be ok. I'm sorry if that's not what you want but this room doesn't have any doors.**

Unfair
Petra Rihan

Keys between her fingers.
Darkness swallowing joy, replacing it with fear.
Am I being followed?
What was that noise?
Fear. Aching, painful, excruciating fear.
Heart racing.
Hands shaking.
Women across the globe have to walk home in
fear of being followed, hurt, or worse.
Sexism is still a raging problem, a cut society put a
plaster over but which is still bleeding. In the
workplace women are still undermined,
underestimated and overlooked.
A man's world where women are still fighting for
human rights. Still hurt over and over simply
because of different genetics and bodies.
You can tell us 'boys will be boys' so cover your
knees and shoulders.
Rip us down, but don't build us back up.
Little girl, go play with your pink barbies, and
dream of being a princess.

People tell women it's their fault for the unwanted baby in their arms, she didn't say no. But you don't know that she tried. Over and over. But you covered her mouth and pulled her hair.

An investigation found out that 97% of women in the UK have been sexually harassed and 96% did not report it because they believed it would not change a thing. There was a trend going round on social media '#NotAllMen'. But if you gave women a box of 10 sweets and one was filled with the most disgusting substance you could think of, you'd be scared of them all. I can't go over every sexist thing done and said. Every snide comment, cat-call, bruise etc.

But I can use my voice, my words.

So go on, society, go on sexists.

Try and stop the fight. The fight for justice, for equality.

Maybe you can muffle our voices with that plaster.

But you cannot silence us.

Queen of Witches
Chloe Pick

It can get very lonely, rattling around my huge house. I remember when Mum and Dad were here. Every day, whilst tea was cooking, Dad would put the radio on and start dancing. He would never stop! Sometimes I wish that they were still here. But I have to forget that.

Remembering pain only makes it worse. And then I would be trapped in it.

All of the big governments think that bombs will solve all the problems they have with other countries but I have a better solution. You see, magic exists and I can use it. Not many people have this power but that's because not many people can say that they have killed their parents. Don't get worried, I didn't *actually* kill them but I *did* accidently let my pet pufferfish, Spike into the swimming pool whilst they were in there. And let's just say that Spike doesn't like sharing his home. To cut a long story short, I was then gifted with these powers. Now I just try not to give into fear and grief that almost drowned me ten years ago. No one knows what really happened to my parents. One of the first things I did with my powers was to make the house look like it had burnt down and that it was haunted. No one has visited since then and I like it that way. But one day, not long ago, all of that changed.

*

I don't know how they found me, but there are people in my home. I haven't seen anyone in my home for ten years. It was too late to use magic to make them forget what they had seen: the enchantments protecting the house had broken for them. Plus I was curious – human interaction was new to me. How do I introduce myself? Would I say 'Hello, this is my house'? But that would lead to so many questions. After all, I was meant to be dead. I checked the security cameras to see where the intruders were. They were heading towards the garden. They would see the zombies if I let them go any further.

I teleported to the intruders, my fists now holding spheres of energy. I had let people think this house was haunted, why not give them a show? I could see now that the two young teenagers who had broken into my home looked terrified, their eyes were wide and they looked like they were about to cry. Perhaps, like the books that I was always losing myself in, they had been dared to come here by their friends. They were even shivering. But that could have been due to the coldness of the corridor we were in.

'Who are you?' one of the boys asked.

I simply tilted my head, my eyes glowing like the flames of a fire. The boys began backing away, fumbling to find the doorhandle into the garden. But I wasn't going to let that happen. If they saw the garden, they would surely die of fear – I'm sure that my poison garden would be a sight to behold for normal people. So instead I drew power from the ancient walls of the building I called home, absorbing the lives of all those who had come before me. I then channelled all this energy into projections of my ancestors. I do believe they would be called 'ghosts'. It seemed to have worked as the boys sprinted away from the door, their eyes frantically scanning the hallways, looking for the way back out.

'I don't quite know why you are running away from me,' I said calmly, flying gracefully across the hallways, batting cobwebs out of the way. They took a sharp right. That would lead them to the garden. Then they would see my parents – I mean the zombies. Why do I always have to correct myself?! Maybe it is time to re-join the world, like the last witch to visit had said.

But there wasn't time to think about big decisions like that now: the humans were almost at the door. So I blasted them. Shot them down. I don't know why. Something overcame me. Something I couldn't control. Hands shaking, I looked around. I had partially blown-up the hallway. I could hear my dogs barking but they sounded so far away. I felt alone. Completely alone. With no one to turn to.

So I healed the boys. They didn't seem too pleased with me as they both scuttled away from me, grasping for the ancient weaponry that hung from the remaining walls. I introduced myself as Elizabetha, Lady of the Manor. They said something along the lines of:

'Argghh… You're the ghost…. Am I dead… argghh!'

Something like that.

But then this happy little conversation was rudely interrupted by an almighty crash down in the garden. That was when I heard the scream. The scream I hadn't heard for ten years. And, just like that, I was seven again, letting my pufferfish into the swimming pool for a quick swim, just like the naive little girl had done so many times before. But it all went wrong.

The little girl was left alone.

All alone.

With no one to look after her.

In that moment, the little girl ripped her own world apart. Her soul had been ripped apart irreparably. That was when I, ten years later, remembered the other person who had been in that room: Agatha. Queen of the witches. And, where she went, chaos and death always followed. I was no longer trapped in that day. I was back in the moment again, screaming ten years of hurt into oblivion, tears streaming down my face, shaking uncontrollably, and being comforted by… humans. All whilst I figured out exactly what had happened, my face a mask that covered the gears and thoughts that were now whizzing around my head.

But for now, I would not be afraid. And I would be the one who watched as she crumbled away into nothing. Then I would rule over the

witches for all of eternity. Queen Elizabetha had a
nice ring to it. Didn't it?

I couldn't stop the wry, twisted smile
that crept onto my face. Oh, things were going to
change on this miserable little planet. And
everyone would know who I was and what the
power of death could do.

You're welcome.

Crying
Eva Maltby

crimson
       creeks
             creep
                down
                      my
                            cheeks...

Dreams before Death
Jeya Sandhar

Blips swished past the monotonous machine, like
eels looking for prey in their homely waters. Each
interval was charged with an electrifying sting,
measuring the pumping of blood, measuring how
long I had left.

The smell of bleach wasn't as strong as
before, the creaking of rubbery pumps echoing
along the hospital corridor quieter than yesterday.

I rested my eyes as a crocus of yellow and
mauve waded into view, smiling in a brave array;
each shimmering cup harbouring a unique flame.
Succulent plants mimicked a border blooming left
and right, adding long forgotten color to my
world that had come to stand dull and lonely.

I wasn't sure how I managed to return, how
I remembered the world of my past that slipped
through the blockades of reality, but I never
questioned it. My subconscious always provided
escape.

Escape from the lingering sense of death

that dutifully hung over my section of the ward.

Laying down, I saw wisps of alabaster smother chirping grasshoppers and paint over the illuminating hues. The fuzziness of new memories could not bother me anymore as I traced the footprints of my past.

The call of a robin grasped my attention but no feeling of want, no need to move could be sensed. A sense of belonging was instilled in my bones, allowing me to rest, to enjoy the time I have left.

Dauntless dandelions flaunted their tooth-like leaves as if to show their fangs were sharper than mine. Show that they were younger and more courageous. My hands moved in tandem with my mind, tracing circles around the stem as an unfamiliar idleness settled in. Clusters of lime accompanied bursts of summer white, decorating the ornamental hedge.

But I still heard faint whispers echoing and oscillating from outside my sphere, repeating the same words over and over:

"Find Dr Hudgeson, my grandpa's heartbeat is weaker… Please, tell him it's urgent."

My eyelids drooped as if they were weights that I had to hold up. The awareness of my limbs was hushed, my muscles resting in the cushion of greenery.

Unsure of whether I was breathing, I lifted a hand to my chest.

Up.

Down.

Up.

Down.

My breath was subtle and gradual. The low thumping of blood was distant, contrasting to the fiery heat that welled throughout my body, taking me further into the comforting abyss that was placed around me.

The Spring Queen's petals stood pale and clean, neither proud nor grand – her feminine touches leaving a subtly sweet scent. The scent known as the primrose.

Pleasant sun rays broke through the haze of unease as I settled for my awaiting slumber.

The blips were subdued, unable to ruin.

A Girl Saved by the Stars
Eva Maltby

Lija finds comfort in the shadows and resists the
urge to stay there all night. There's a cool breeze
coming in from the east and it pinches her cheeks
ever so softly, she can feel them going rosy. The
not-so-distant rumble of thunder makes her pick
up the pace and soon she finds herself entering a
tavern. It's relatively empty, save a few old fools
drinking their sorrows and those serving them.
No one sees Lija as she climbs the battered
staircase and enters the first-floor flat.

The baby lies in the middle of the room
and Lija watches as he shoots a hand into the air
and grasps a non-existent finger. Lija lurks for a
while in the corners of the room where the light
from the fire doesn't quite reach. She observes
what little one can of the new-born child. She
watches the way he swings his limbs in the air,
sucks his lip, scrunches his face.

As it approaches midnight Lija emerges
from the corner and stands in the middle of the

room. She glances out of the tiny wooden-crossed window. The sky is perfectly clear at this precise moment, and she admires her decision to make the stars bright tonight, showing anyone who would notice, this is a special night indeed. She doubts anybody but the old man in the astronomy tower will notice but he won't live long enough to be able to put two and two together. Besides, people always forget to look up.

Lija places a steady hand on the baby's chest. His breathing calms and he lets out a gentle sigh that makes Lija's heart stutter. The new parents lying in the bed beside her stir but do not wake and Lija is thankful. As she whispers to the baby, she hears the patter of droplets on the window and the soft shake of thunder. The deed is done. She glances out of the window again; the stars are covered by clouds now and a wave of disappointment hits her. It would have been nice if tonight her stars could shine uninterrupted, but she sees that this storm is too strong to move on in the few hours of darkness that is left. She begins to leave but just before she does, she leans over the cot where the baby lies and cradles its head in her warm hands.

"Remember, the stars still shine in the

day, even if you can't see them," she tells him softly. Then she plants a kiss on his forehead, surprising herself. The baby smiles and she smiles back at him, wishing him the best, then wishing her wish could be granted.

In the next village along, a lady sits on the side of the road sinking into the rain. She cradles her new-born child in her arms, sheltering its face from icy knives. She shouts and cries, but the winds sweep her voice away and up out of earshot. Finally, she wishes, she wishes this storm would stop, she wishes for her baby to survive the night, she wishes for the gods to protect her baby girl. She screams to Lija, Goddess of the Stars and Granter of Wishes to help her and her baby.

As Lija shuffles out the door of the tavern and into the rain, the lady's wishes reach her. She is feeling kind tonight and grants them. The rains slowly begin to ease, the skies become silent and the clouds depart leaving Lija's stars for all to see. The lady stops crying and lifts her hand away from her baby's face. She notices her child's skin is no longer blue but lively pink. The baby is smiling, and the lady can't help but beam. She tilts her head up to the sky in joy and notices for the first time how beautiful the stars are tonight. The lady knows Lija has answered her wishes and made the stars shine. And Lija is right, the old man in the astronomy tower does notice how bright the stars are tonight and she is right that he does not live long enough to join the dots, but the old man isn't the only one who sees the stars. The lady decides right there and then her daughter must be called Aster: a girl saved by the stars.

Happy New Year
Fanni Doroti Polgar

"Happy New Year," is what everyone says.

"Happy New Year," I say to myself, because deep down I know that there's a lot to celebrate. Fireworks, party hats, banners and a glass of drink sitting in front of me. It is one hour to midnight, and the clock is ticking in a manner deliberately obtuse.

I'm standing on the carpeted floor of my bedroom in a knee-length cerulean dress, sleeves puffed and a jazz record running recurrent laps around the turntable; every possible thing in place to make me feel as though I am living in the decade I wish I was born in. A decade in which struggle was real, but so was life, the music, the stories, the food, the passion, and human communication. The time before artificial ideologies began consuming young minds in the form of phone screens. The time before fake became the new real...

I contently live out my fantasy, with equal optimism in my thoughts and words so much so that the only open door from here is disappointment. Just as I begin to believe that this night could not get any more comfortable, a friend calls, as she has done every year:

"Happy New Year!" is what she would always say. But not today, not this year. She tells me that a friend only months older gained wings and arrived in heaven just moments ago. I cry for her, I speak for her, I try to make a sound. To break the silence. So that she knows I am here even when the whole world has blacked out.

Twenty-nine minutes to midnight.

I put the phone down, and the drink stares me in my eye. I hate that drink. I hate the taste. I know I hate it because I've forced myself to try it every year. But, still, I grab hold and take a sip anyway.

And another.

And another.

"Happy New Year," is what everyone says. But tonight has made something wistfully clear – happy is only in the phrase for some. Why do some get to stay when others have to fly?

Does it make me a fool to feel *happy* tonight?

Human
Fanni Doroti Polgar

Suffering presents itself in too many colours to
comprehend,
in numbers greater than what words can
express…

Knowledge of others enduring more
doesn't make your struggle valid any less.
Yet struggling more than another man
does not mean your life isn't blessed.
Stop the comparing;
pave way for the sharing.
For beyond all we are the same in one
immeasurable existence:
human.

Painting Pathos
Fanni Doroti Polgar

There is power within pain; there is pain within power. And there comes purpose from the power of pain…

Humans are ever so fragile. We begin as sinless seeds, grow our roots, and begin to blossom from the emotional torment of circumstance. It is quite tragic how our character is shaped more by sorrow than jovial memory. Nevertheless, that is simply the way in which the world turns.

Few of us admit to being broken; few of us admit to allowing pain to define. Instead, we stare at a blank canvas, four vacant walls; a lifeless vision from ceiling to floor. We stare until the wisdom born of wounds pierces purpose through us – we begin to paint our pathos. We paint a lifetime.

Inadvertently, our paintings turn our isolation into inspiration, our pain into passion, guilt into gift, trauma into treasure and sadness into success. Each painting unites to fill the lifeless walls with significance and comforting colour.

We begin painting from as young as every morning sun and carry our canvas into our futures; writers, actors, artists, leaders, teachers, doctors, nurses, dreamers – we create a world of meaning, where we raise our children to never stop believing.

We must let it be said that without the power of pain, neither I nor you would be who we are today.

Summer clouds
Emily Lonsdale

The clouds are a mundane shade of grey when we make our reunion.

Which is perhaps an inaccurate reflection the energy rippling through my body in the form of foot-tapping and frantic checking of an internet messaging application.

We have plotted, schemed and connived to be here at this particular location and this particular time: quite a feat for a group of teenagers whose primary skills rely on speed typing, an exploit organised entirely online.

We have bludgeoned our way through the online booking process and several re-scheduling phone calls to finally make this date, not a week after we last saw the same sweaty summer faces. The place is strange to every one of us but is about to become irreversibly entwined with an early summer experience where at long last the mock exams are far behind us and ahead, an isle of artificial grass and poor-quality golf clubs.

We unite, perhaps not with the hip nod of the head some may expect from the teenagers lurking at Broadway but with laughs and cluttered smiles, my father now resigned to take the bus alone as I join the group to light-heartedly bully a latecomer by phone and groan together as our enquiries are met with vague promises of being nearby.

I attempt to tug away feelings of being undeserving of such mind-blowing excitement; the gap between our last meeting and today is such a small margin, but I'm caught up laughing once again as the latecomer makes their entrance to innumerable sarcastic remarks: "Merry Christmas!" Now we've been brought together, I can only think that that week of holiday was the longest I've felt in a while and surely I'm right to bring such a broad smile to this rare event where we don, not uniform, but t-shirts with online tickets waved high.

There is precious little room to reflect as we roar in honour of unexpected deflections and defective putts on the space-themed greens, but I catch the gleaming eye of a pal and once again feel as if the world is at our feet – or at the very least confined to my rubbery ball and a third slice of pizza.

It continues even as light drains from the sky and we take to one side: food consumed, mugshots perused and removed quickly from chats even as we sit across the table from each other.

Explaining yet another tale of somewhat embarrassing woe I'm certain I've told before, it's difficult to think that in no more than month or two I will be through with being fifteen and move on to the more responsible end of being a teen, but perhaps this can wait just five more weeks. Perhaps I can hold on tight to these score sheets and my lack of responsibility. Maybe that's just it. I don't need pathetic fallacy to support my enjoyment of these last few weeks before it begins.

Day Three: ALTER EGOS

We asked our young writers to imagine an alter ego for themselves, complete with their most distinctive character traits, and build a story around them. They chose styles and genres they thought fit their alter ego character best.

The Skyrush
Hattie Payne

The sun blazed in the pale blue sky, not even a wisp of white in sight. The heat was suffocating, like a pillow, soft but deadly, smothering everyone and everything. Sweat coated my skin; my clothes clung to my body like a child to their mother. Beads of sweat trickled down my face too, but I made no effort to brush them away. My head hurt, my neck hurt and even my eyes hurt. I was so tired.

Sleep crusts were building up in the corners of my eyes, blurring my vision and defiantly staying put when I tried to rub them away. The skin underneath my eyes was tinged a horrible colour that was a blend of purple, blue and grey. My hair clung to my neck and back. With long, nimble fingers, I twisted my chestnut curls into a bun and stuck a hairpin through it to keep it in place. My hazelnut-coloured skin glistened in the golden light that bathed the ground in warmth and my eyes drooped. I was *so* tired.

All I needed was rest. I wanted to crumble to a heap on the cobblestone street and sleep for a hundred years. But I couldn't stop. I forced my limbs to work. I made myself put one foot in front of the other, again and again, even when I thought it would kill me to do so.

My attempt at navigating the spiderweb of streets was useless. They all seemed the same to me. Twisting and snaking lanes of beige-bricked cottages all crawling with ivy, vine or wisteria. The gardens all looked the same too. Vegetable beds, a tree here and there, flowers, fruit and greenery. I could've sworn I passed the same house five times.

For a while, I refused to give in. I refused to face the facts. But after a few hours, when the sun was slowly slipping over the horizon and the sky was painted in colours of rose, violet and gold, I gave in. My spirit crumbled. I was *lost*. Dreadfully, hopelessly, desperately *lost*. My legs gave way beneath me and I collapsed onto the floor. My knee seethed with pain. I pressed my hand against it and lifted my palm up to my face. It came away a deep, crimson colour.

I stared at the pavement as my vision fazed in and out. I sincerely hoped that someone would come along and find me, but, then again, I didn't want anyone to discover me. They would think of me as weak and there would be so may questions - *too* many questions. The last thing I remembered hearing was footsteps on the street behind me, and then the world faded away to nothing...

*

I was woken up by a cold draught creeping over me. I shivered. Goosebumps prickled across my skin and all the hairs on my body stood on end. I scowled through closed eyes. It was definitely not supposed to be that cold.

I could no longer feel the cobblestones underneath my body. I was lying on a smooth surface. A *wooden* surface.

My eyelids fluttered open and I gazed at my surroundings in shock and terror. *Where was I?* It was a cold, dark, damp room. The walls, floor and ceiling were all made from dark oak planks of varnished wood. It was void of any furniture or decoration but for a large crystal chandelier. The little beads of transparent crystal on it clinked against each other. There was a strange hum coming from beneath me and a gentle rocking motion that soothed me for a minute.

The calming effect quickly wore off. The beads of the chandelier were still clinking but now it was menacing, their rhythmical music like a clock, ticking away at the seconds I had left to live. Bubbles of panic grew in my chest, bursting like the bubbles my little sister used to make back home. *Home.* Where was home? Where was *I*? *Where was I? Where was I? Where was I?* I tried to calm myself down-to burst my panic bubbles as if I was popping them with a needle — but it was no use. I felt overwhelmed by everything. I lay there, curled up in a tight ball like a cat, shivering in fear. My whole body shook, but I wasn't sure whether that was from the vibrations below me. It probably was. I was like that for hours, the jostling movements below me causing me to repeatedly knock my right hip and shoulder against the floor.

Eventually, my panic eased away – like the tide edges away at the rocks near the bottom of a cliff – and I was left with the ability to think in my usual logical trail of thoughts. *Right*, I thought, *what do I* know? I *knew* that I had been moved from where I had blacked out and I could *guess* that I was on a boat or airship or some other large moving vessel.

I got to my feet and looked around the room. There seemed to be no door, but my eyes quickly picked out the amber outline of a large rectangle set into one of the walls. I caught a flash of something else too. Metal? It was metal, but not just any metal. Hinges! And a lock too!

I darted up to the door and rammed against it with my shoulder. It wouldn't budge. Locked. Why did they always have to be locked? Luckily, locks had never been much of a problem to me – and they most certainly wouldn't be now!

Crouching down, I examined the lock. The key was still in the other side and twisted. I pulled the hairpin and a hairgrip out of my curls, letting them fall back over my shoulder blades. I tucked a strand of hair behind my ear and got to work. Using the hairpin, I prodded the key out of the lock. It fell to the floor on the other side of the door with a loud, echoing clank. I winced, waiting for the pounding of footsteps outside. None came. I slotted the hairgrip into the lock, and after a moment or two of fiddling, I heard a loud and satisfying click. I stood up, allowing a small smile of self-congratulation to creep onto my lips. Using my palm, I pushed open the door (it was soundless - the hinges well-oiled) and stepped outside.

I expected my feet to find a long, winding corridor, but I couldn't have been more wrong. I emerged into a large room with a long, rectangular table in the centre. Seated on either side of the table were about fifty men in smart, entirely black and white suits and colourless ties. All eyes were on me. I felt my heart thump loudly in my chest. By their sides were dreadful cutlasses. *Pirates! Oh no, oh no, oh no! What have I done*, I thought, panic building up inside of me.

"Good evening, Aria," drooled a falsely sweet voice at the head of the table. "You made quick work of that lock. Impressive."

My eyes flickered over to where the voice had come from, and once I'd seen it – or rather, her – I couldn't tear my eyes away.

At the head of the table stood a formidable looking woman with tanned skin and cropped golden ringlets of hair. She was tall and slender with broad hips, a square jaw and sharp cheekbones. A glistening cutlass hung at her waist, but that was not the thing that scared me the most. The most frightening thing about her was her eyes. They were blue, and at a glance they seemed quite ordinary, but the harder I stared, the eerier they looked. They held no warmth whatsoever. They were the same blue you might expect to see in a frozen lake, the sort of lake that when the water touches your skin, you know you'll die before you feel the sun warming your back again.

The edges of her mouth lifted in a sickly-sweet smile and she flashed her pearly white teeth at me. Her smile was like honey and I was a fly caught in her trap.

"Welcome aboard the Skyrush," she said. There was an aura of menace around her. Her whole body radiated with it.

I gulped. I did not like it. I did not like it one bit.

A fearless recklessness coursed through my body. I lunged for a cutlass, snatching it up and brandishing it in front of me. My heart hammered even louder in my chest. I couldn't breathe properly, it came out too quickly, too sharp and too snappy. My chest heaved with terror. I couldn't think straight. I couldn't think at all. I doubled over, clutching my side, my eyes wide. I was panting so heavily. My heart was thumping wildly in my chest now; my vision blurred. *Was I about to die?*

I knew the moment had come. I had to do it. I let determination and courage surge through my body like wildfire through a cluster of brambles. I felt something fizz in the tips of my fingers — something coursing through my veins as easily as blood. I crouched down, my knees bent, my head tilted towards the ground with my hair like a curtain shielding my face and the tips of my fingers brushing the wooden floorboards. A splinter pierced my skin, but I wouldn't feel the pain until much, much later. I leapt into the air, and for a moment I felt like I was flying. The air around me shimmered with a mysterious golden light. I could not see the pirates at the time, but now, when I imagine them looking at me as I jumped, I see them gawping, mouths hanging open.

When I touched the ground again, I no longer had hands or feet. My hair was gone, my ears were no longer rounded and at the sides of my head, nor was my nose slightly pointed at the tip and curved upwards ever such a little bit. The only things that remained the same were my eyes - an emerald and a sapphire set into my face.

I loved my new form. I loved the way my

triangular ears would twitch at the smallest noises, and the way my long tail curved upwards in a curious question mark when I was happy. I loved the way my face looked as though it was split in two, with the right side as white as snow and the left as dark as midnight. At the base of my neck, the black furs overtook the white, leaving the rest of my body, mainly the colour of charcoal, with a white chest, socks and tail tip. *I was a cat!*

I darted under the table and quickly emerged out the other side. Out of the room I went and into a corridor, darting past rows of doors. As I sprinted up onto the deck, a wave of cold washed over me. The deck was huge! Probably as big as my village back home. Above me were three giant, cream-coloured balloons and thirteen vast, indigo sails. To my left and right were great wings of the same purple but patterned to look like feathers.

I changed back in to a human and dashed for the railings. My stomach lurched, giving a little flip. I threw up over the side. I was flying low over a dark, stormy ocean. Waves crashed into each other, raging war. The sea churned white foam that even from that height licked my face like an excitable puppy. I tasted the brittle, salty ocean air on my tongue and vomited again. The rocky cliffs of Mainland were not too far away but were becoming more and more distant by the second. If I jumped there and then, I could probably make it to shore. *Probably.* My heartbeat quickened and quickened, until it no longer had a rhythm to it and was just a painful throbbing motion in my chest. My lungs heaved, gasping for air, as five large, muscular men in impeccable suits and the woman emerged from below. I had made up my mind.

I vaulted over the wooden railings and plunged down and down. For a few blissful seconds I felt like I could grow wings and soar through the sky. Then the force of the fall hit me like a smack in the face. Pain and agony stampeded through my body like a herd of frightened elephants. The bitter cold clawed at my skin, the nails of the invisible hands that were dragging me down into the darkest depths of the ocean. My eyelids fluttered, half open half closed. The world swam before me as the current tossed me around. I lost all sense of direction – up, down, East, West, they were all the same to me. Eventually, the water spat me out. I landed with a heavy thud on a cluster of jagged rocks. I began to roll back towards the sea, its malicious fingers trying desperately to reclaim me. My hand found a grip in the rock and I caught myself just in time. With shaking limbs, I pulled myself onto a flat surface, and lay there shivering and panting like a dog in the hottest days of summer, for what felt like eons. My clothes and hair were waterlogged, squeezing my frame tightly. My eyes stung with salt water and my mouth, nose and ears were full of it. The ocean gushed out of my mouth and trickled down the side of the rocks, leaving me with a sick feeling in the pit of my stomach.

Then I realised something. I was free! Excitement and relief quickly consumed me and the empty feeling vanished. I was free!

I quickly crawled back into the ocean with my new-found strength. With flailing arms and kicking legs I swam to the cliffs and dragged myself out of the water. As I looked up at the cliffs I felt quite terrified, but I now know I oughtn't have worried. I quickly grew into a rhythm of hand, hand, foot, foot, and by the time I reached the top, I could move without even thinking.

Soon, I would realise that I was, in fact, not free, and that I would spend many more years running and hiding. But for now, I'll let my twelve-year-old self celebrate like there would be no tomorrow, dancing and leaping on the lip of a cliff.

*

Carved into the rocks high above the murky water is two words. These two words tell a story. Perhaps it is one you've heard or perhaps it isn't. It is the story of a young girl who could turn into a cat and who escaped from the clutches of evil many times. Carved into the rocks is a name: Aria Dewdrop.

Crestan Café Murders
Sadeen Ahmad

I had always been told that people pitied me; they
looked down on me with forged frowns and
tissues all too saturated with 'tears' once they
heard the wildfire rumour about my parents. I had
always been mocked for dressing with long skirts
and full sleeves. But do they really know what's
concealed behind them? That the long skirts are
just a show, a camouflage? I had always
compressed those tongues of fire within me, not
just from the mockery, but from people's minds.
Because I can read them.

Minds are the place you can see what raw
and honest opinion people have of you. That's
why I gave up having friends such as Ruby and
ending up trusting no one and evading all
mankind. Knowing that I can read their minds,
their 1-star ratings of me, how they really just use
me like a rag doll and call me a freak. They don't
know I can delve into their thoughts and minds
and therefore just fall, unbeknownst, into my plan.

Like always.

Never in my lifetime, did I think that I would reveal the magic I could do, the stash of weaponry strapped to my knees or the genuine reason my parents died. I haven't even told Ruby about it. But I guess the Crestan Café really does hold victims, witnesses, accusations, and, of course… murderers. You may see me as an ordinary schoolgirl, waiting tables, who's really a freak behind it all. But what if I told you: I'm just there for the show. I'm *really* a detective. Someone who solves murders, crimes and gets to the bottom of messy business. I've been trained from birth and this is the one exciting thing that I have left. By being seen as a peculiar person, with no friends, I don't call anyone's attention. But that's part of the plan. And it gets even more intense.

As I hastily make the numerous orders of coffee and banana muffins for tables 4 and 6, I stare at the old man sitting on the windowsill, hidden by the ivy decorations and drinking from a steaming mug. I've never seen him before. It's strange though, he asked for multiple shots of espresso and ordered the coffee so bitter and strong, I wonder how he drank it. All I know is that you should never mess with someone who drinks strong coffee; it adds to their personality. Zapped back into the present from my suspicious thoughts, I walked off to serve tables 4 and 6.

The next second, he was gone. No mug or money left and no sign of him. Something was wrong. Something was terribly wrong. Then I heard a scream. Piercing the air like nails and hushing everyone in the room. I dropped the mugs of coffee on the ground and raced behind the counter, but when I entered the pantry, I couldn't take another step. My stomach lurched and my was head spinning.

Ruby was there. Lifeless on the ground, head flopped to a side and blood flowing profusely from her head. Next to her was my boss: her eyes bloodshot with tears, her head shaking side-to-side and trembling. She looked up at me and screamed again. *My daughter. My daughter.*" Was my bosses daughter my 'friend'? Why didn't Ruby tell me? What happened to her? Where's the old man? And… did I just fail to stop a death?

Always Running
Khadeeja Irfan

The bus ride home was stressful. I spent the entire journey wishing the bus to go faster. I needed to be away from society as soon as possible; by now they could be on my tail! I was rerunning the course of the day, mulling over the events, fermenting my anger. It had all started in the morning: Form Time ran smoothly and then the deputy had come in asking for me to make my way to the head's office. Palms sweating, knees shaking, I left the classroom visibly worried, leaving the calls of my classmates behind me.

"Ooh, you're in trouble..."

"Ooh, what did you do this time..."

I made my way to the Head's office feeling as if I was in a dream. The walls were definitely caving in, the floor was definitely moving, and my breakfast was definitely about to make a reappearance.

Palms sweating, I left. They were going to tell Mum; I was going to kill Randy. He said it was secure, he said no one would ever find out, he said I'd be okay. He said, he said, he said, HE LIED! I was going to find him and wring his neck, all the while listening to the cracking of his bones and squealing of his cries. Or I would shoot a singular bullet straight through his skull – but he deserved something a bit more dramatic, something that would strike fear into his heart, something to make him call for Mummy before taking his last breath.

Oh, I was going to enjoy myself. I always knew it was a bad idea bringing in a civilian, but however much I told them the more stubborn The FIRM became. Passing a mirror, I slowed, realising I looked as mad as I felt. I was red, eyes bloodshot fists clenched, hair tousled, and I had been running. I wasn't going to take my time; I had to complete my mission and then disappear. But it wasn't going to be as difficult as it seemed. I was an expert. I had done this all before…

The Phantom
Blake Scammell

The lights in the vaults dimmed. The guard on duty frowned before checking the control panel. She frowned even more intensely. The lights were on full power, and yet were dimming significantly. She made a mental note to alert maintenance to the faulty lights. Little did she know that she would never remember the lights in wake of the events that followed.

She heard a loud *click*, and the steady hum of an opening vault door. She spun around, but there was nothing there... and yet the only way to open the door was via the control panel.

And that's when the lights went out.

She was blinded by the darkness, stumbling frantically, trying to find the control panel in the inky black void. A shape flew by in the darkness. She squinted, desperately trying to make out whether the shadow was something more corporeal.

Suddenly, a foul odour invaded her

nostrils, and she fell to the floor. When she got up, the lights were back on. The vault was open.

And the diamonds were gone.

The police investigation was a sham, a failure. *They were bumbling fools*, thought the thief. *They cannot account for the unexpected. And nothing is more unexpected than instant darkness, conjured by me. Now for my next plan, I need to be incredibly precise, or else it will not succeed.*

He adjusted his black gloves, and began to write down the particulars of the next theft…

The police were baffled over the string of strange robberies that had occurred over the past few months. The victims were all rich, pompous, unlikeable characters with ludicrous amounts of money, all of whom had lost at least half of their millions. The thief had several trademarks: They always struck in between 3-4 AM, they had a device which could somehow dim and turn out lights, they managed to disable CCTV cameras by flooding the room with something that was so dark that the CCTV could make out nothing more than a dim shadow, and they were striking in a circular pattern around the outer layers of London.

By using this pattern, it was possible to predict who the next target would be: the notorious businessman Joseph Malton, who was nearly universally disliked because of his nasty habit of financially destroying his rivals in the clothing industry. His fortune was somewhere in the billions, making him a prime target for the mystery thief.

Mike was attending the police conference on the burglar known as "The Phantom". He had been the first to arrive on scene at the latest attempt, where the thief had gassed the guard, knocking her and the CCTV out, opened the door via use of the control panel, and escaped with half the Hurlerson fortune. It would have been his friend David who answered the call that night, but he had been stuck at home with a nasty case of the flu and unable to return to work.

David, who was sitting next to him now, asked Mike "Do they have any idea who the culprit is? We could really use some leads…"

"No, whoever they are, they have a method of disabling CCTV that is so effective that it's impossible to make out anything more than a patch of darkness on all the recordings from the thefts." Mike returned to listening to the conference.

David looked nervously at his watch, and adjusted his black gloves…

The next time The Phantom struck, the police were ready. There was a guard force of twenty trained SWAT team members guarding the entrance to the Malton fortune from midnight to ten in the morning, and police officers surrounding the entire building. Every nook and cranny was full of bugs, CCTV, and anything else that offered a chance of identifying The Phantom. Mike was among the officers selected. David was as well. They guarded the building and the priceless fortune it held within for the entire night, until the police chief was satisfied that it was past the time where The Phantom would consider an attempt on the fortune.

"Well, good to see you guys haven't been slacking while you were guarding my fortune. I must say, you've done better than I expected," congratulated Joseph Malton as he opened the heavy vault door to his fortune. "I mean, I guess having SWAT operatives counts for something, but –"

The vault was empty.

David chuckled so quietly that nobody else

could hear him. The problem with police is that once they see a pattern, they never forget it, and they forget that others can change their behaviour. *They also never suspect one of their own,* he thought to himself. *The amusing thing is, having taken the fortune before they expected, they've been guarding an empty chamber for ten hours. What a waste of time and manpower. And now for my final heist…*

Three days later, the police were still utterly bewildered, attempting to work things out, when the news came in that a total of a couple of billion pounds had been donated to the NHS, anonymously. The only person who had the money and was even remotely likely to donate that amount was The Phantom. The police were even more confused.

David smiled quietly in the corner. Surprising, how misjudged some characters can be until the end.

And that was the last anyone saw of The phantom.

A Good Murder Mystery
Angelica Hadjianastasis

It's another busy day in the bustling city
that Emma Disaster lives in. The sky is grey and
foggy, the happy energy of the sun nowhere to be
found. She completes the same, mundane routine
that she does every day to get to work: get up, get
dressed, leave the apartment, walk to the train
station, get something at the nearby *Marks and
Spencer*s for breakfast, and hop on the train for
work. Boring, right? Well, that's life for you.

Emma chooses a cow print coat for today's
wacky outfit, grabs her keys and leaves her 1-
bedroom apartment. She buys a jam doughnut
from the Marks and Sparks on platform 3 and sits
on a bench waiting for the train, which is late, as
usual. She looks over and sees two people sitting
on the bench to her right. One of them is dressed
in a forest green puffer jacket and jeans, and the
other in a silky, scarlet red dress.

Considering the enthusiastic conversation
they're having, they must be going somewhere

together, making at least one of them in a completely wrong outfit for the occasion. Well, Emma isn't wearing the most normal choice of clothes either, so who is she to judge? The train has finally arrived, so Emma steps on, the people in the green jacket and red dress following behind her. She takes a seat and they sit opposite her, still talking to each other.

Another man in a mustard yellow striped jumper and round tinted glasses sits a couple seats away from Emma. A woman in a plum purple pencil skirt sits a short distance away from her, on the other side.

"Morning" the woman gestures politely.

Emma smiles back at her. The carriage doors close so that all of them are together in the carriage. Emma sits there as the train starts moving, reading a book on her phone, when suddenly, the train drives into a tunnel, and the lights cut out. She tenses up and hears a gasp from the direction of the woman in the red dress opposite her. The train goes so silent that Emma can practically hear the racing heartbeats of everyone in the carriage. She grips her seat as the train rides over a bump, something that would've been unnoticeable in a normal situation, but feels amplified in this moment of tension.

The second they leave the tunnel, the lights turn back on, revealing that the person in the green jacket is lying limp on the seat, eyes rolled to the back of their head, tongue lolling out, bleeding from the chest. As soon as she sees this, the woman in the red dress lets out the most ear-splitting scream and bursts into tears, causing her mascara to run and her lipstick to blot. Emma leaps to her feet, as does the man in the yellow jumper.

"I'm a nurse. I can check what happened to them and clean up the wound," he says with a sense of level-headedness in his deep voice that calms the other passengers, Emma included.

She decides to talk to the woman in the red dress and ask her what happened.

"I-I don't even know! I saw the same as everyone else here, lights going out and then coming back on to reveal my best friend dead! DEAD!" She screams the last word with utter grief, and Emma feels a pang of empathy for this poor woman.

"Sorry to interrupt, but this person has clearly been stabbed," says the nurse in yellow.

Emma's eyes shoot to the woman in red,

the only person who could've killed them in such a short amount of time.

"It wasn't me!" she shrieks, "I would never do that, and I couldn't even fit a knife in this tiny purse anyway!"

Emma looks to the purse, and agrees that it is far too small to fit any fatal murder weapon.

The woman in the purple skirt stands up. "It's in her bag! You can see the metal knife shining, sticking out the zip!"

The woman in the red dress pulls out the knife and gasps. "It wasn't me! Someone must have snuck this knife into my bag! I bet it was her." She looks at the woman in purple.

Emma looks at her too, and notices something on her arm. The lady in the purple skirt sees it too.

"Wait, I—"

"No need to defend yourself. We know it was you, because of... THIS!"

Emma grabs the woman's arm and holds it up for the others to see, revealing a spot of deep red blood, hardly dry yet, contrasting against her crisp white blouse. The woman stands there shaking, unable to get any words out. Her mouth hangs open as her breathing quickens irregularly.

The nurse in the yellow jumper is already dialling 999.

"Wait," Emma says, "Before we jump to conclusions, I'm taking everyone here to the police station."

The woman in red's eyes widen. Eventually, everyone agrees. The woman in the purple skirt seemed oddly confident for someone who was so suspicious. Later, at the police station, the group were sitting around waiting for the DNA results to come back. Finally, a young-looking police officer came back with the knife in a zip-loc bag. Everyone sat up.

"The results are back... the murderer is..."

The women in the red dress and plum skirt were tapping their feet the loudest of the group.

"...Bianca Peterson."

There is an assorted mixture of confused sounds. Nobody had actually caught anyone else's name.

"Who is that?" the man in yellow asks.

The woman in the red dress gets up confidently. "Fine. It's me. I killed them."

"B-but why? Weren't they your best friend?" Emma asks.

"Of course not. I was only trying to get

close to them for their money. I wore a red dress to disguise the blood stains, so I could blame it on the fool who decided to wear white," she glanced at the woman in the purple skirt, then at Emma. "I suppose I underestimated you, Disaster. I wasn't expecting you to take it this far, to take it to the police station."

Emma smirked. "What can I say? I love a good murder mystery."

Life
Umar Arshad

Soaring in the idyllic sun-streaked sky was a bird, its wings outstretched and its feathers glistening.

Leaning on a smooth oak banister down below was a figure, a no-faced figure with no eyes and a body made entirely of white milky mist. It looked up at the bird longingly, for it was trapped on the earth, unable to thrust itself into the air and outstretch its arms to reveal silky geometric patterns of feathers, could not use them to glide as far and as wide as it pleased with the gale brushing its face.

The figure then got up and walked away into the dark cavern of loss, and when it did, it felt the strong gust of despair trying to blow it apart. The figure strained to keep its fluctuating body together by thinking of the bird; eventually the wind passed, allowing the spectre-like humanoid to continue.

Almost an hour later, the figure had

reached the Asylum of Manipulation, named so for its mistreatment of those who dwell inside; turning their slight issues into monstrous beasts. It had to go through there, it had to.

As the ghostly figure slinked itself through the labyrinth of a structure, the rusted flaking iron chains clanked against themselves in the roof above the hospital-like halls, ghastly wails of agony ricocheting across the white marble walls. Just then the cracked white lights flickered a bit, before blacking out entirely, leaving the figure in a cold black hysteria of fear.

As its dread got worse, it started to feel the gust of despair again, slowly but steadily ripping it apart, as the flailing spectre began to adjust its vision, it saw goliath beasts, their obese folded skin a sickening yellowish white with bright scarlet liquid leaking out of their ligaments, some parts of their body ripped revealing blood-stained bones.

This horrific sight caused the gust to blast off entire chunks of the figure's body and into the dismal abyss behind. It tried thinking of the bird. How it wanted its place and how happy it made it to imagine being the bird. But it didn't feel any better, the winds kept on mutilating and disfiguring it, until it realised that in order to feel content, it had to satisfy itself with being itself: a unique work of art.

And so it did. *Click.* the lights switched on and revealed a safe passage to the exit of the asylum, and no leviathan beasts to be seen.

Years have passed. Our figure has been permanently changed since the asylum, obviously it has aged but it has also changed in other ways, for the asylum made it realise it was enough, and since then the cavern of loss was not so bad and dark and dismal as before. In fact just up ahead was a giant opening in the cavern roof revealing the bright light grey sky and letting in the fresh pure breeze of content.

And so finally our figure, our spectre, our ghost has reached the pinnacle of its life; it has grown up and escaped the cavern of loss and reached the cavern of endurance.

Day Four: LETTERS

We asked our young writers to
address a letter to an inanimate
object, abstract concept or their
future selves.

Dear Writing

Fanni Doroti Polgar

Dear Writing,

It's strange to think that of all letters I've ever written, this is the one I've found it hardest to find words for. I found you, or should I say: we found each other, when I most needed to be found. You took the timid, adrift, six-year-old me and taught me a new language, introduced me to a new world and with that new world, gave me dreams and a purpose. You became my escape and my outlet, during the trouble and the tidal tests; you stayed even for the brighter days and the happiness.

You, writing, are the one passion that has never stepped out of fashion, the one dream that has never faltered, and the one thing that has never made me doubt my ability. You gave me a voice when I needed one; a voice that I could raise before I was comfortable showing my face.

You introduced me to fiction, in which, over time, I discovered my own fact.

Writing, I've grown up with you and grown more in love with you as time has gone on. You've never given up on me. So now, in this letter, with these words that mark the page: I promise to never give up on you…

My Dragonfly Earrings
Iona Mandal

> *The pair of silver dragonfly earrings that kissed my earlobes like a rose's thorns, harsh yet forgiving.*

To my very own earrings,

When you first met me, I was a bawling, dribbling mess. Talcum sobs and milky burps escaping my lips before your involuntary penetration. I treated you with distaste. The first entity which had dared to maim me since birth. How dare you trespass the cloudlike lining of my skin and make it your own? Invading and subduing a powerless wretch.

The ear-piercing specialist pierced one of you too high, almost as if you begged to straddle the gulf between lobe and bone. To this day, I resent you, even a little. Though I have grown to understand that all of us are selfish in our own ways. You, too, were once merely a nymph. Hindwings still fumbling for grip, weak in the lifelong rat race for growth. Pulsating thorax resting upon my ear, as you whispered little witticisms, travelling through my nerves like cable lines. If I was quiet enough, I could hear you breathe, hear your eyes, far too big for your face, blink like the release of a raindrop.

We were both naive back then. You thought your flight had no limits and I believed you would never stray too far from my reach. We were both mistaken. Many a time you fled from the boundaries of my ear, snuggled away in the seams of a cushion or the loops of a gold chain directly beneath, as if retreating from the prison-like abode of my cartilage. But I learned to love you. Cherish the sinful glint you gave to strangers on streets, the way your abdomen gleamed under the mid-April sun, the translucence of each cellophane wing.

I must admit, the idea of replacing you had never quite fled my mind. Emerald teardrops and opal hoops lured me with the deception in which they caught the light. Something you only did when you felt like it, dulled by years of dirty bathwater and accidental misplacement. But nothing quite spoke to me like you. In the end, it was you who found your flight. Years of dormancy, tamed by the domestic life of an ornament, rusted your unwilling antennae. This life was never for you, trapped and frozen into nothing more than a cosmetic plaything. Culling the unpredictable trajectory your life could have taken, like the grey dotted lines in picture books.

You lived up to who you are, dear friend. A symbol of change and self-realisation. New growth fuelling you through the metamorphosis that sought to please none. Perhaps you are still there, somewhere, within the fibres of a fleece coat. Or in the pearl box beside the bathtub, I never bother to check. A speckled bus floor or shadowed crevice. But something tells me you have finally become who you truly are, gained physicality and drive. No longer tucked in the hole of my ear, but between the spores of a dandelion, being the accidental pollinator, you are.

With love that took me long to muster,
Your grateful ex-companion.

Dear Earth
Petra Rihan

Dear Earth.

I'm sorry.
I'm sorry we've pulled up your roots.
Torn away layers and layers of your life
Burnt your heart for our homes and pathetic
pleasure.
I'm sorry I forget about you every time I secure
my seatbelt.
I'm sorry I don't appreciate every season that
passes year after sorrowful year.
I'm sorry your eyes have been clouded by thick,
unforgiving fog. You can no longer see.
You can't feel because we've scorched your fingers
with our forest fires,
You can't breathe because we're drowning you in
an ocean full of polluting plastics.

I'm sorry because our governments don't listen.
And every change in everyday life I make is just a
plaster covering one wound in a war full of

wounds.

I'm sorry they're not listening to your agonizing, deafening screams for help that echo off our crumbling walls.
I'm sorry time is running out and that you try and you try but they fight and they burn your fossil fuels and cut your trees and let our factories clack and clog away.

I'm sorry. I'm so sorry.
From, one mere individual.

the Sea, with love, Ophelia
Eirini Vassilas - Smith

I look out into the
  murky waters, leaning over
    the cold edge of the boat,
forcing it to tip
slightly.

Don't
  do
    that,

the voice
in my head says.
I ignore it   and lean over
Just a little   further

stretching out,
  my fingers craving touch.
I want to lean out,
to fall in,
to die in this

beautiful place. My hand
meets the sandpapery
skin of a whale.

They're
    actually
dolphins,

intones the voice in my head.
 The Orca below me
    makes a strange noise,

beautiful like a Siren's song.
It occurs to me now that those
    poor, lonely
    sailors who claimed to hear
mythical beings and got nothing
  but sneers in return

    really were hearing mystical
   creatures, these strange things,
  and the love songs
  they sing each other.

 My fingers pass over the handsome,

perfectly carved fin
as he passes   so elegant,
  breathing his salty-hot mist up at me.

Gentle   beast

    I whisper as it calls,
the strange echoing cry again.
It seems lonely.
I wish it could fix that.

Maybe.

I lean further in
pulling
    Down
        the boat
so that the edge skims the very waters.

I long to inhale the water
        look out, and see
 the light, dancing in strange pattens above,
 fill my lungs
 with something that
will be the death of me.

Are
  you
    sure?

It's very peaceful here.

I look up at the sky
          and I think
      that if the sky
   and the glassy sea
swapped places

I would hardly tell
  the difference.

Both are midnight blue, both
draw me in, make me want to
leap forwards,
          be absorbed in their quiet
depths forever.

Day Five: FISH OUT OF WATER

We asked our young writers to write a piece featuring a character in an unfamiliar world, or write the beginning of a story in a new situation without giving the reader a long backstory.

MI6's Imaginary Worlds
Sadeen Ahmad

What is this place? Why are there little kids scrambling around this confined room? There's pink everywhere: flowers that are painted on the peeling walls (showcasing its mustard and mouldy figure), crayon drawings etched violently in the stacks of paper, now left with shreds and pink remnants, and paint flying off saturated brushes. Great. There goes my new blazer.

Where am I? What is this prison world of mini-me's screaming for no reason and laughing maniacally when smearing paint on my face? Ugh. There goes my nose. As I walk (and tread on the creepy-eyed dolls that these 'people' are crushing to death) I sigh in relief. A door: an escape from these Munchkins. As I reach for the knob – also smeared in pink – my slow-motion reflex kicks in and it takes a few seconds…just before I feel an aggressive snag of my shirt and my head smashes into the knob, knocking me out cold.

As I groggily and forcefully open my eyes, I see the toddlers all assembled into immaculate lines 4 by 3. Their big doll eyes glare like sharpened knifes into my soul. Then they smile: simultaneously and still reverberating that disturbing side of them. I panic: I've faced immense rivals, advanced and impossible-to-escape weaponry and I've faced savage escapades. But never has James Bond. Me. Myself. And I. Faced insignificant children. Their innocent exterior is a mere illusion to their controlled, creepy interior. As I struggle, succumbing to the knots of rope intertwined between my legs and arms, I realise that this is yet another mission. One with no backstories, explanation or help. Just me. James Bond. Confronting robot Munchkins who are hungry to capture me and do some more.

"What do you want from me?" I say, faltering with every word.

"We know you are scared. But don't worry, we only want you to play with us and stay here forever. We shall have the best of times."

"Let. Me. Go. Then… I'll play with you." I lie.

"We know you're lying. You're going to run away, aren't you? Out of that door, back to your world."

"You mean, this is a different world? This

was a mission and I can escape from that door?" I blurt out.

"Yes. But this is not a mission. It's a test from MI6. Let us see what you do, to innocent children like us."

"Well," I chuckle, "three-year-olds don't talk like the Queen. You're a robot, an illusion. And I can harm you."

I lift myself up and smash the chair on their bookcase as it feebly falls to the ground. I snatch the ropes off my body and run like never before to the door. The children leap on me but miss by mere seconds. I kick it open and all I see is the sky. So, I leap, pulling my emergency parachute in my pocket. I see my world and twist backwards to air blow a kiss to the Munchkins. Just another imaginary CGI world by MI6. An impressive one though. And I turn back around and laugh. Laugh maniacally because I just defeated children. *I guess I really did smear pink paint in their faces.*

Tintin in Tibet
Iona Mandal

Tintin's ginger quiff had been almost completely covered by snow, to the point where orange streaks peeked out like he was a frozen orangutan or something. He had been trudging through the Tibetan mountains for hours now and the snowstorm did not seem like it was ever going to end. Just as soon as he thought it was on its way to subduing, alas, another snowflake made its presence known, covering another patch of the flame-like projection upon his head. Tenzing Dakpa was just a few metres in front of him, always keeping close watch so Tintin would not lose his way in these treacherous conditions.

Snowy had been for two hours now. No amount of clicking, barking or yelling showed any sign that he was still in a mile's radius and Tintin was on the verge of going nuts. His one true companion, the creature he trusted more than himself had left his side. And it was all his fault for not being more careful in the depths of the snowstorm. How could he be so stupid? After all, Snowy was the perfect candidate for a thrilling game of hide-and-seek in a storm of the precipitation which his very name was derived from. He must have lost his way in the few moments when Tintin was not keeping a death grip on him.

It was hard to tell what time of day it was. The sun hardly ever made his highly anticipated guest appearance in the unbearable theatrics of pretending to appear for a moment but sneaking back behind the clouds. No Yeti, Bigfoot, Abominable Snowman or any other variation of the creature they had been dreading and yet almost hoping to come across. Just the bleak landscape that enveloped all, smothering them with the desolate reminder that the open jaws of Mother Nature really was no place for a whimpering puppy.

Even Tenzing Dakpa was starting to get fed up now, and every few minutes, he would mutter something under his breath about foreigners being ignorant. Still, they had a long way to go before there was any sign of civilisation that was not inhabited by a hostile old man in his pathetic square metre of a hut. Tenzing knew these mountains like the back of his hand – where the yaks gathered and black-necked cranes nested, what season you would find a blue bear and even the exact location of some of the oldest cypress trees in the area. Tintin, too, trusted him blindly. But what worried him most was that Tenzing had never been on edge before. Emulating the hospitable spirit of his community, he always treated Tintin with utmost respect and patience, sympathising with his lack of experience, but admiring his courage. Today was the very first time he had expressed even a hint of impatience and this reaction had undeniably stirred Tintin. Were they ever going to find a way out of this perilous land?

Just as they were relying on the last ounce of hope, it flashed before their eyes like the uproar of a flame before it dies. If he squinted hard enough, in the distance, he could just about see a slightly larger shack, the most noticeable thing about it being a very red front door. Though Tenzing was still quite a distance in front of Tintin, he had not seemed to have caught on yet – the biting cold and burden of a lost dog – convoluting his mind. Tintin immediately called out, informing him of the discovery. And he responded with a brisk nod of approval. A few more minutes of trudging through the dense snow and they were at the red front door, golden murals they had not spotted from afar, now greeting their vision.

Despairing as they were, Tintin offered to knock first, desperate for a hot drink and perhaps some help finding his poor, misguided companion. Snowy's loss was becoming ever so prevalent, and he already missed hearing the playful yaps of his furry friend, a pleasant change from the hissing gale and white noise of the peaks.

Knock, knock.

No response.

Knock, knock.

Silence.

Knock, knock, knock, knock. He was getting impatient now.

Still nothing. But a faint muffling on the other side, as if someone was fumbling for keys.

With a reluctant creak of the door, out came a hunched figure, mostly toothless and with a quivering voice. He seemed to be taken aback at the sight of a foreigner traversing these harsh lands, yet almost gave a nod of approval in seeing Tenzing.

"And what do you two want?"

"Don't talk to them like that!" a warmer voice resounded from behind.

"There's a crazy blizzard out there and you expect me to be friendly?!" the hunched man responded.

"W-well, you see...we were just wondering if...hot drink...shelter…" the cold had partially numbed Tintin and he couldn't find the words to continue. Tenzing Dakpa stepped in, speaking in a torrent of Tibetan, until the hunched man sighed and reluctantly let them in, nudging a glass of hot yak milk towards them, as if he was being forced to.

Tintin was still curious about the warm voice that had been coming from further into the shack. It sounded very vaguely familiar, somehow, as if something he had once heard on television or radio. That kind of mellow, yet cheerful tone that assured you of being in safe hands. As the hunched man from before crept back to the kitchen, Tintin bravely ventured to the corner in which he heard the voice coming from. Tenzing seemed to be too enthralled by the sensation of warm yak milk running down his throat to care, and what met Tintin's eyes next, filled him with disbelief.

His saffron and red robe was masked by the thick fleece that hugged his shoulders, but the keen smile as he looked up from his cup of steaming butter tea, immediately confirmed Tintin's suspicions. Upon noticing the classic gold framed glasses resting on the bridge of his nose, Tintin gave a gasp. It was none other than His Holiness the 14th Dalai Lama! What was he doing in the Tibetan mountains? As far as Tintin knew, the Dalai Lama lived in the hillside city of Dharamshala, far away in India!

And even after a good few seconds of being stared at in utter disbelief, he seemed to retain the same expression of contentedness.

"Would you like to take a seat? You look ever so cold," he uttered softly.

"A-ah yes, of course. I just was not expecting to meet you here...today... of all places!"

"Oh! So, you recognise me!" he chuckled. "Well, you see, I am here visiting a distant cousin of mine. Nothing more than a little reunion. Now tell me, what brings you here?"

Tintin was not sure how to approach a man of his stature, but his friendly nature was impossible not to give in to. And so, he went on to explain the purpose of his visit and the tragedy of Snowy getting lost in the blizzard, with regret.

The Dalai Lama stopped for a while to think. He seemed to consider it a part of his responsibility to help those in need, or those suffering from loss. Briefly clearing his throat, he began to speak:

"There is a well-known Buddhist parable I think may help you. A very long time ago, there was a very wise man. A man we all know. His name was Siddhartha Gautama, also known as the Buddha. Now around the same time as he was living, there was a woman named Kisa Gotami, who was in a bit of a pickle, you see. Kisa's only child, a very young lad, had died.

"Unwilling to accept his death, she carried him from neighbour to neighbour and begged for someone to give her medicine to bring him back to life. One of her neighbours told her to go to Buddha, located nearby, and ask him if he had a way to bring her son back to life. Bringing the body of her son with her, Kisa found Buddha and pleaded with him to help bring her son back to life.

"He instructed her to go back to her village and gather mustard seeds from the households of those who have never been touched by the death. From those mustard seeds, he promised he would create a medicine to bring her son back to life.

"Relieved, Kisa went back to her village and began asking her neighbours for mustard seeds. Unfortunately, although all were willing to give her mustard seeds, they all told her that their households had been touched by death. They told her, 'The living are few, but the dead are many.'

"As the day became evening and then night, Kisa was still without any of the mustard seeds she had been instructed to collect. Kisa realised the universality of loss. With this new understanding, her grief was calmed. She buried her son in the forest and then returned to Buddha to confess that she could not obtain any household untouched by death.

"Though I am sure nothing nearly as morbid has happened with your delightful friend Snowy," he chuckled, "I want you to know that loss is universal."

Tintin was lost for words. He usually never knew how to react to such profundity. But with a sigh and a final gulp of warm yak milk, he thought he finally understood.

Alligators on the Nile
Blake Scammell

It was a normal winter evening, and I was on a
river cruise down the Nile, one of the most famous
world rivers, and the longest. I had had enough of
the nail-biting frost and searing winds back home,
not to mention the lack of snow, and had fancied a
trip to Egypt during the winter. It was cooler than
the Egyptians were accustomed to, it being an
uncharacteristically cold winter, however I was
perfectly at ease with the warmth. After a trip to
the pyramids, and a glance at the world-famous
noseless Sphinx, I decided to take a river cruise.
The Nile is famed for its length, its role in ancient
Egyptian economy, and its crocodiles and
alligators. I boarded a cruiser of the finest quality
for this venture and set off down the river. It was a
perfect evening, an idyllic location. Absolutely
nothing could go wrong. Until it did.

The first I knew of it were the yells, and
the bloodcurdling screams. I quickly turned
around from my midnight cup of coffee to see a
scene I will take to my grave. Terror coursed
through my veins as I saw the alligator finish off

what was left of him. THERE WERE ALLIGATORS ON THE BOAT! My heart pounded out of my chest as I started to run. I ran as fast as I could, running till I was sure I was at a safe distance. I ran to the captain's cabin, gasping and wheezing.

"What's going on out there?" he demanded. "All I can hear is screaming!"

"There-" *gasp* "-are alligators-" *wheeze* "-on the boat and-" *gasp* "-and they're killing people," I panted.

The adrenaline was still pumping in my veins, draining my normal calm, controlled self and replacing it with someone who was terrified and had no clue what they were doing. The captain's calm, controlled voice brought me back from the brink of a mental breakdown.

"We get everyone to the lifeboats and abandon ship. Are you listening?"

"Yes. Just panicking for a minute."

He seemed to understand. "I'll rouse the crew and passengers. Make your way to the lifeboats yourself."

I took his advice and ran. A few minutes later, everyone who was left had gathered at the lifeboats, and we left the ship. When lives are at stake, there is no point to worrying about what will happen to a vessel, so we left it. I decided to spend the rest of my holiday in a different climate with less alligators. However, that didn't go particularly well either…

Runaway
Petra Rihan

We are all lined up in the grand hall of my family's castle.

Woman after woman.

Hair tied in elaborate styles, dresses of numerous colours in all types of outrageous fashions. Mother hosted a 'proper etiquette for women' class, which I was forced to attend. But my mind had no space for posture and manners, for it was racing with thoughts. I am going to leave today, run and never stop. Escape this prison.

My own gown of silk is a pale purple that disgusted me, and my dark brown hair in an unnecessary updo.

"Jane, straighten your back!" Mother snaps at me. A burst of giggles erupts from a few girls. I roll my eyes. Pathetic.

"My back is fine, thanks." I make a note to slouch further.

"Well, it's time for tea and biscuits, then we

should get back to it." Mother claps her hands, and the girls go off on their own.

It's time.

I walk out of the hall, unseen, slipping through the crowd of ladies.

I scan the room, and see my pre-packed bag hidden between two disgusting, expensive ornaments.

I untie my hair and braid it into a simple plait before taking off my tall heels and replacing them with a pair of sturdy boots.

Good. The window is open.

Of course it is, it's a warm summer day, in which no girl should be wearing their over-the-top gowns and be forced to be cooped up in this palace.

Lifting my skirt and stepping onto the table, I climb through the window. The forest is so close, I simply need to run.

I hitch up my silk skirt, and tumble from the window. I clamber up, quickly, and run as far and fast as possible.

My skirt billows in the wind, my legs a blur. I laugh wildly as the forests envelope me and I continue to run. Everything has gone to plan.

I stumble over branches, slip over rough

roots, but keep running even though my chest is searing with pain. I know the village is to the left, and it's only a short ride by carriage.

However, I need to go forward.

I can't believe I've finally done it. I've got away from that grand, marble, overgrown place. Slowing down, I see Lavender Lake. A fitting name. The water glows purple, and a lavender scent sits in the thick foggy steam it emits.

I walk across the log that acts as a bridge.

I came here as a child (when I was trusted on my own) to get away from life.

I decide to sit and rest, letting myself sink into the bushes for a minute.

I have a plan.

I'm just not sure if I can pull it off.

The Queen's Adventure
Angelica Hadjianastasis

Lizzie woke up with a start to find herself
snoozing among dusty cardboard boxes, instead
of her usual queen-sized bed with luxury silk
sheets and a floral duvet. She stood up and tried
to wipe down her expensive gown. It was
probably contaminated by poor people to the
point where she would have to burn it as soon as
she figured out how to get back to the palace.

Looking around, she came to realise she
was in some sort of storeroom. Listening hard, she
figured out that it was the storeroom of a shop,
straining her ears to hear the frequent beeps of the
cash machine. Don't ask how she recognised this
sound. Lizzie was a people's girl once.

She pushed open the heavy storeroom
door, which was the most amount of work she had
done since World War II. Upon first glance, she
realised she did not fit in with the people here. She
immediately shut the door again and shuffled
about to find a worker's uniform. She picked one

up that had the worst stench she had ever had to encounter in her life. It was probably her size, not that Liz ever used normal clothes sizes, all of her attire was custom tailored for her. She reluctantly changed out of her usual dress into this poor people's wear.

The logo was not one she recognised, but underneath it read "Poundland". Lizzie thought she had heard this somewhere but wasn't too sure. She didn't use normal shops. Her personal shopper went to a private Waitrose for her. Pushing the door open again, Lizzie realised she would have to face her fear of the working class if she wanted to get back to Buckingham palace. They couldn't be that bad, right?

She exited the storeroom, expecting at least some form of acknowledgement from the others in the shop, but everyone simply continued with their day without a second glance at her. How did nobody even recognise her as their queen? Was the uniform that bad?

She composed herself and simply tried to walk smoothly to the exit, in the hopes that people would give her only as much attention as when she left the storeroom, so she could try to work a modern telephone and call her chaperone to come pick her up. She skillfully dodged past avid shoppers, displays of shampoos and stacks of toilet roll. She was almost there; she could see the light...

...until someone tapped her on the shoulder. She jumped out of her skin at the feel of someone touching her without her strict permission, hardly stifling a shriek.

"Oi, where do you think you're going? Your shift isn't over yet," he paused to read her name tag, "Lexi."

Lizzie was taken aback at someone speaking so rudely to her, telling her what to do. She had to try not to blow her cover.

"Uh," she stuttered, trying to disguise her posh accent with a Brummie one, "I was just going out for a... smoke."

She guessed that that was what the youngsters got up to these days. The worker looked her up and down, judging what to do.

"Alright. Five minutes. Now go before I change my mind."

Lizzie exhaled in relief, thanked him and left the shop as quickly as she could. She looked around for a phone booth but couldn't see one on this street. They'd clearly become a lot rarer these days. Lizzie wondered why that would happen, surely people still needed to use them?

After two minutes of very hard searching, she found one and called her chaperone. He picked her up in her vintage mini and drove her to Buckingham palace, where she took a three-hour-long bath to clean her of any poor people's dirt that may have contaminated her.

She recounted the story to the rest of the Royal Family and they praised her for being so adventurous and doing so much hard work. She went to her bedroom, telling everyone that she would burn the worker's uniform. When she got there, she decided not to destroy it. It was a reminder of today's adventure and she felt she should treasure it. She chucked it in the laundry basket for someone else to wash.

Word by Word
Fanni Doroti Polgar

'Primary School' is what the sign reads, but the letters don't piece together words that I understand. Ever since taking my seat between those two broken wings, the world has become one I don't understand. My two small hands mould around my mum's arm so tightly that I see her fingers turning from pale to pink to purple; my palms become submerged in too much sweat to swallow, forcing my grip to succumb to defeat.

I fall half of my height in distance, and the landing stabs holes in the sides of my shoes; saving the gaps to hurt later on. My only focus is on suppressing the ocean from spilling out of my eyes, and mum takes care of picking up each piece of me in her arms. She transforms my small steps into metre strides, and I suddenly feel twice as tall. The world feels a little safer up here. It feels a little more familiar…

A single memory later, we arrive outside of the gates, revealing a painfully perfect line of

with meaning. Letter by letter. Word by word...

Two halves of a caterpillar
Eirini Vassilas-Smith

Scars fade

that's the point
a fresh wound
the drip
drip
drip
of blood onto the floorboards
a sound that calms the caterpillar

but sets it on edge
at the same time
time
time
fades
That's the point.

Another year.
The cocoon hatches

And then a click
click
click
Of cold moments

Brushing by her open eyes.
A sound.
The sound
sound of the creature's wings
spreading as she cautiously
takes flight. That sound
calms. But darkness
is drawing nearer.

And the fact that it is coming
sets her teeth on edge
edge
the eggs on the edge
of the leaf begin to come to life
she is on edge as she watches

their fate has been settled
the tap
tap
tap
tap

of nails against
fragments of glass skin
the caterpillar splits.

Two halves, both dead.

Surely Dead
Petra Rihan

My feet… Why are they so cold…?
I gasp as I wake from my prolonged slumber. I've
been running for days and needed a break… I
didn't expect to fall asleep. I try to figure out my
surroundings, but it's so dark in this forest.
I'm tangled… I slowly begin to realise.
My feet are in the river I fell asleep by last night. I
must've slipped. I try to pull my legs free, but
they're stuck.
My heart begins to thump. This isn't good.
The moonlight finds cracks through the
intertwined tree branches, and it shines on the
river. It's eerie.
My arms are trapped, tangled within brambles
and roots.
I try to wriggle free again, but I slip further. From
my torso down, I'm now in the river, getting
tangled in weeds.
I'm shivering from the ice-cold water.
A lump rises in my throat and I want to scream,

but I need to stay calm. Something shifts under my back, and gravity gives way. My arms get ripped from the sharp plants they were tangled in, and I whimper. Suddenly, I'm rapidly sliding into the river.

I take a deep breath.

I drop.

Body submerged.

The icy cold water shocks me, and I lose sense of where I am.

I can't breathe.

My feet are stuck.

I'm trying to swim to the surface, but it's too high, so far…

I'm light-headed from panic and lack of oxygen.

Weeds slow me down as I reach for the dagger on my belt.

I feel for my feet and start cutting around them blindly.

But it's too late.

My arms go limp as I desperately try to free myself.

Icy water fills my mouth as I scream.

My chest aches for air.

I see stars.

Then, I feel my dagger hilt drift away from my

hands.

It's over.

I'm dead.

My hands scrape uselessly, weakly, at the soil by my feet.

Suddenly they're free.

…Huh?

I can barely move, but I muster up the last bit of energy I have.

Land.

Air.

I cough, and water dribbles from my mouth.

I shiver uncontrollably.

How am I not dead?

I collapse.

Breathe. Just, breathe.

Spark
Young Writers

Creative writing groups for children and young people in the West Midlands

£90 per year
£9 per session
Aged 8–17

Supported using public funding by
ARTS COUNCIL ENGLAND

WRITING WEST MIDLANDS

www.sparkwriters.org

Printed in Great Britain
by Amazon